Once there were **3** little

   named Tipsy,

Topsy, and Tim. They lived

with their  in a wee

tiny  on a  .

One day a came

from their grandmother.

In the  was a

for  , a  for

 and a and

pair of  for .

The  put on their new clothes, and didn't they look grand! cat said, "I'll make brand new for all of you."

She finished them that very week:  for Tipsy, for Topsy, and

🧤 for Tim. The 🐱🐱🐱 were very happy and proud as Punch of their new 🧤.

They wore them day in and day out, but one day they came to 🐱 with 💧💧💧 in their 👀. "We lost our 🧤," they sobbed. "Oh dear, whatever shall we do?"

 was busy making

a . She turned

around quickly, and

scolded, "Lost your

you naughty s!

Then you shall have no  ."

The    wiped their   with their   and went to look for their  . They asked

if she had seen their , and next they asked the playful if he had carried them away.

"Cluck," said . "No, I did not see your ."

"Bow, wow! No!" barked the playful . "I did not carry away your ."

The looked on top of their s and under

their s. Finally they looked in an old full of clothes in the attic.

"I don't see how they could be in this ," said .

"We haven't been in the attic for weeks."

said, "We haven't been anywhere except the woods to pick for 's ."

"And that's just where they are!" squealed .

"They're hanging on the

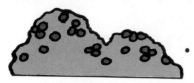. Don't you remember we had to take them off in order to pick the ?"

The 🐱 🐱 🐱 hurried to the . Sure enough, there were the 🧤

hanging from the 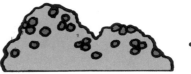 .
The 🐱 🐱 🐱 put them on
and ran home to 🐱 .
She was so glad they
had found the 🧤 that
she gave them the 🥧 .

"It's the best  I have ever eaten," said 🐱.

"It's the juiciest 🥧 I have ever eaten," said 🐱.

"But look at our 🧤," said 🐱.

The  🐱 🐱 🐱 ran to 🐱 and showed her their sticky messy 🧤. "You naughty 🐱 s!" scolded 🐱.

So again the 3 little s began to . After a while  said, "Let's wash our messy  and then they'll be just as good as new!"

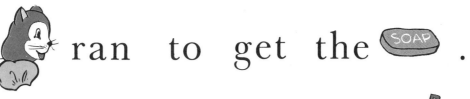 ran to get the 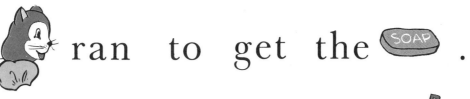 .

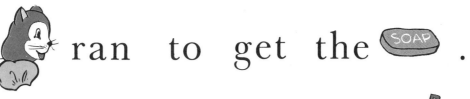 ran for the wash ,

 brought out the

 and the .

They filled the with

water and made lots of

 suds. Then they threw

in the and scrubbed

and scrubbed and

scrubbed until the

stain had disappeared.

Then the s hung their on the clothes line to dry. Soon they were soft and fluffy and dry.

The  ran to .
She smiled at wearing
her blue , and at Topsy
with her red and
at with his bright
yellow . She said to

them happily, "You are the best s in all the . Now let's all be very quiet, because I smell a close by."

The 3  tried to keep still, but they were so happy that they said, "Purr, Purr, Purr!"

THE THREE LITTLE KITTENS

Here is a poem about the Three Little Kittens
for you to read and learn.

Three little kittens lost their mittens,
  And they began to cry.
"Oh, Mother dear, we sadly fear
  Our mittens we have lost."

"What! Lost your mittens?
  You naughty kittens!
Then you shall have no pie."
  "Me-ow, me-ow, me-ow, me-ow."

The three little kittens
  found their mittens,
  And they began to cry,
"Oh, Mother dear, see here, see here,
  Our mittens we have found!"